Don't Make Me Act A Fool

by

Michelle White

ENAZ

Don't Make Me Act A Fool.

Copyright © 2009 by Michelle White

All rights reserved by the author. No part of this publication may be reproduced, stored in a retrieval system or transmitted in any form or by any means electronic, mechanical, photocopying, recording or otherwise, without the prior written permission of the Publisher.

For more information, address:
Enaz Publications
P.O. Box 030064
Long Island, N.Y. 11003

Cover designed by CSO, NY

Library of Congress Cat. Num.-in-Publication Data

ISBN 1-59232-169-0

Printed in the United States of America

Dedication:

I dedicate this book to my sons, to my Aunt who pushed me to make this dream a reality, to my sister, and my best friend, for listening to everything I had to say, to my family, my spiritual parents and my church family, to my friends old and new, to the person who influenced my life the most, my mom who is no longer with us, but forever in our hearts, Know that your baby girl took a chance and saw things through to the end.

Have you ever been so pissed off, where you're about to explode. The stress is building up, and you're about to slap the hell out of anybody who gets in your way. Your parents are driving you crazy; your sister is a pain in the neck, and your lying ass boyfriend should have got the boot months ago. The only sane person in your life is your best friend, but you both are about to drive each other crazy if you have to listen to each others' problems one more time.

All I can say is keep pushing me to the edge, and I'm About to *Act A Fool*!

Table of Contents

Part One

Frustrated and Tired.................................... 7
I Get What I Want.. 12
What They Don't Know............................... 18
Summertime... 23
A Party Aint A Party Till I Walk In................. 28
Class Is In Session....................................... 33
Birthday Girl... 37
Love Me or Leave Me................................... 42
Here We Go With The Drama....................... 47
Girls Just Want To Have Fun......................... 52

Part Two

I Swear To Tell The Whole Truth.................... 59
I'm Not the One to Judge............................... 64
Quiet as It's Kept... 72
Why you Wanna Act Like That...................... 78
Can We Talk for a Minute?............................ 82
Finally We Agree... 87
This Is Who I Am... 92
Roses are Red... 98
Patiently Waiting... 105
I'm Finished.. 110

Michelle White

Part One

Frustrated and Tired

Damn, its 2:00 in the morning why in the hell is my phone ringing. "Hello." "Meshay, I'm sorry." "Whatever, Damien, I'm done with you." "Man, come on, quit tripping, Meshay." "What?" "You sleep?" "Yes, Dame, what do you want?" "Baby, I love you." "Damien, you don't love me." "Man, I know I messed up, but baby you know how the game goes, you forgave me before so why can't we get back together now?" "Oh you really don't want me to answer that."

I knew Damien wanted to get back together but I wasn't ready. I was tired, tired of his bullshit. I was starting to really see that Damien was so full of himself, and his lies finally were catching up with him. I was fed up with this relationship, and I wasn't going to continue to allow Damien to play me for a fool.

You see my parents were real old fashioned. They wanted me to make better choices, and that's why we always disagreed on the friends I had and the guys I was into. My father, Richard, worked at a nightclub, and my mom, Beatrice, worked for the Police

Department. I have a younger sister, Mechelle, who is two damn grown for her age.

After I graduated from high school, my mom retired from the Police Department. She put in 25 years--she worked in the Community Resource Intervention Department as a supervisor. Her job was to supervisor various programs throughout the community. These programs were for ex-gang members, teenage mothers, single parents, and at-risk teens.

Even though my parents had enough money to pay for my out-of-state tuition, they convinced me to stay in town for college. I was spoiled--I knew it and my parents knew it. It was a four-year difference between me and Mechelle. Once Mechelle came along, I still didn't see why I shouldn't have my way--I mean they chose to have another baby.

My parents had become uppity--for years we struggled. I grew up in the hood like everybody else. I knew what it felt like to be broke. I had my fair share of bologna sandwiches, noodles, hamburgers with white bread, and Vienna sausage instead of hot dogs, because they were cheaper.

My dad worked at Clovers for 15 years before they made him co-owner, and they only did that because he invested so much money in the place and kept it going. When the city decided to shut it down, my dad paid the money to keep it open. He worked as the bartender, on the door, and he even started a restaurant in the back. Before his restaurant, the place had less than 100 people each week.

My dad was older than my mom by 15 years, so he was set in his ways. He was a real good chef and my mom was a great cook too. I learned how to cook from the both of them, so I would help out as well. Once things started to pick up, my dad ended up buying the nightclub.

That's when all the changes started. I was in the 8th grade and my parents decided we should move. I was glad because I would no longer have to share a room with Mechelle. My parents were finally buying a house. To my surprise, it was out of the ghetto and into some bougie neighborhood. To make matters worse, they felt me and my sister should attend private school. I would have to spend my whole four years in high school at some College Prep Academy. I was so hurt. I would have to leave all my friends behind to make new ones. These were my friends since kindergarten.

Even though we lived in a different neighborhood, my mom still chose to work in our old neighborhood. She did love her job, and she said "I'm not trying to forget where we came from, I'm just trying to show you guys there is better opportunities out there."

So now the only time I saw my old friends was when I went to help my mom out to the community center. Since both my parents worked, I never could get a part-time job in high school. I was only able to volunteer through my mom's job.

That's how I met Damien. He was only 18 and I was 16. Although my parents said I couldn't date until I was 17, I knew I wouldn't be able to date Damien at all. Damien was enrolled in one of my mom's programs. I swore Damien was about 20--I mean he was fine, tall, thick, chocolate complexion, and had a low fade. He had about 10 tattoos. I loved tattoos. I couldn't wait until I turned 18 so I could get one--I wanted a butterfly right across my left breast.

Even though Damien had just got out, I don't think he left his lifestyle behind him. He had an old-school mustang with candy paint, rims, and the beat. So he either had the car before he got locked up or recently purchased it with the money he had saved. I knew he had some saved up because he would always be fitted when he came to the center. His hair was always cut and his clothes were name brand. So I knew he probably wasn't so willing to give up his lifestyle.

I Get What I Want

I remember the day I met Damien. I was pulling up at my mom's job with my dad in the passenger seat. He finally let me drive his baby which was his black Mercedes 500e class. What he didn't know was that my mom let me drive all the time as long as she was in the car. I had my permit but my dad felt I wasn't ready for his baby, and my mom's convertible Volvo was good enough to drive.

"Meshay, don't park right here, I don't want one of these little thugs to mess around and hit my car with one of those handballs." "Daddy it's not nice to call people names, you can't assume everybody that come to the center is a thug." "Whatever, they are--thugs, ex-thugs, same thing." "Daddy, I'll go get mama and you can stay here and babysit your car". "No, no I will go and get her, so you and her won't take all day, I know you want to see if your little friend Shooboo is in there." "It's Shabria or Bree."

I waited in the car for my parents to come out--I decided to let my Dad drive us home. As I was getting out the car, I noticed the ball coming towards my direction. "Oops, my bad." "Please tell me you just didn't hit my daddy's car with that ball." "Ain't no scratch on it, it's cool." "You don't know my daddy, it is not cool." "How about you give me your number, and I will come over and wash your dad's car and buff out any scratches I may have caused."

"You must not know who my mom is. My mom is Mrs. Lewis." "Oh, Mrs. B is your mom." "Yeah" "No disrespect, I'm Dame, I mean Damien Waters." "Hi Dame, I'm Meshay". "Yo mom's is cool, real cool. I'm in her program, she been helping me out a lot. "So why are you dressed like that, you on your way to church, you in the choir?" "No, I just came from school. "I attend Benjamin Franklin Academy." "Dang, like that--bougie all day--hood at night." "Whatever." "I'm saying though, you keep it real and you educated. That's cool. Well let me go, it was nice talking to you Ms. Lady, and I hope I can get that number next time." "Who says it will be a next time?" "Oh trust Ms. Lady, I will see you again."

"Meshay", who was that boy, you were talking to?" "Oh daddy please, some guy in one of mama's programs. "I don't even know him, his ball bounced by your car and I got out to catch it before it hit the car." "You know how I feel about these knuckle heads around here." "Yes daddy, I know." "Richard what are you fussing about now." "Hi mama." "Hi Meshay." "Daddy was tripping because I was talking to one of your students."

As we were driving home all I could think about was Damien. I knew in a million years my parents would never allow me to date him. I wondered if maybe he really wasn't all that bad, I mean he was in my mom's program, so maybe he was trying to get his life together. I don't know what made me interested in him, but I sure was going to find out something about Mr. Dame.

RRRRRRing. "Hello." "Shabria, who is Dame?" "Meshay, please don't tell me you met Damien". "Yes, and girl he is fine." "And an asshole too." "Shabria, you say that about every guy." "Well it's true." "Well I want him." "Be careful what you ask for." "You know your parents ain't about to let you date him." "Please, I will be 17 in a few months. What they don't know won't hurt them." "Okay Meshay, you gonna mess around and get your virginity taken and end up pregnant." "Come on Shabria, all I want to do is talk to the guy."

"Well Damien ain't no just-talk-to type of guy, he the type of guy that will talk you right up out of your panties." "How you know?" "Meshay, you act like I don't see him all day, everyday flossing thru the hood. Have you seen his car?" "Yeah, I just left my mom's job." "Okay then, how you figure an 18-year got a car like that?" "I know, I know, but he said he was in one of my mom's programs." "Probably the one for ex-cons, he was locked up for a year." "So everybody deserves a second chance."

"Okay girl, just be careful. You still coming over this weekend?" "No, I'm babysitting Mechelle." "Damn girl, isn't she 12-years old; she can stay home by herself?" "Please, that brat will have burnt the house down. So you come and keep me company while I baby-sit." "I don't know maybe, your sister get on my nerves." "Like your brother don't work mines." "Who Steven"? "No, the older one." Oh girl, you know Shaun is in love with you." "Shabria, your brother is 21-years old and still has no job". "Girl he slang dope like the rest of them." "Okay call me tomorrow." "Bye Meshay." "Bye Shabria."

"Meshay come downstairs, your daddy wants to go over the house rules while we are gone." "Mama how long have I been watching Mechelle?" "Baby I know, but this is the first time we will be gone for a whole weekend, and Las Vegas is not that close. You know your daddy will have a fit if he had to fly 400 miles, then turnaround to have to come back early."

"Don't just walk in my room." "You better not ignore me this weekend to hang out with yo hoochie friend." "Mechelle, shut up, you always gotta start some mess." "Mama, Meshay is being mean to me." "You little brat." "Meshay, don't call your sister that."

"Alright, here it is—Meshay, you are not allowed to drive neither one of the cars, only one person can spend the night, no other company besides that one friend, your mamma's friend, Rebecca, will come over to check on you. You have the numbers in case of an emergency?" "Yes daddy, and what about Mechelle? You need to talk to her; she got a real bad attitude." "What about you, Ms.Thang?" "Mama, I'm almost 18 and about to be grown." "No Ms. Thang you are almost 17 and still living in my house."

"I can't wait till I leave for college." "That's if you even go somewhere." "Mama, what did you say?" "Nothing, we will talk about it when we get back."

What They Don't Know

My parents were on their way to Las Vegas, and I was stuck as usual babysitting Mechelle. I was glad that Shabria decided to come and spend the weekend. As I was waiting on Shabria, my mind started wondering about Damien. I had to find a way to run into him again. I didn't want to start going to the community center because my mom would get suspicious. I hadn't been in a while and really hadn't had any extra time.

With me graduating from high school, I was so busy filling out applications for college and looking for internships or volunteer work at a school. I wanted to be a teacher, so any experience would look good on my college applications. I knew my parents didn't want me to go too far, so I only applied for one out-of-state college, which was Alabama A & E.

My next two choices were Fresno State and Sacramento State. I figured they would at least let me go to either one of the two. I had family in Sacramento and Fresno. I was really leaning towards Sacramento. My uncle Raymond and my aunt Brenda and their two daughters Tanya and Aisha lived there, as well as my Aunt Cathy and Uncle Jeremy and their daughter Rayne

My Aunt Pamela, Uncle Aaron, and their daughter Shawna, and their two sons Corey and Pierre lived in Fresno. My Uncle Raymond's son Michael and his wife Cassandra and their three daughters, Destiny, Valerie, and Tierra lived in Fresno too. The rest of my family lived here. My mom has four sisters and four brothers. They are Allen, Craig, Josephine, Raymond, Belinda, Cathy, Roman, and Pamela

My dad had two brothers and one sister. They are Travis Larry, and Mary. I only met my uncles once when they came to California, they were from Chicago, but I never met my aunt. I did meet my dad's cousin Pearl when she came to visit.

My family on my dad's side was small, and on my mom's side it was medium. I always enjoyed our family gatherings, which would be held at our house most of the time. My mom would cook these big meals; it was always plenty of food. Although my dad was the chef--he was trained in the Army and traveled all over the world--my mom still did most of the cooking. That's how I learned, but my dad could make the best barbeque, and his sauce was the only sauce I would eat, and I don't even like sauce on my ribs.

I knew exactly what my parents wanted to talk about. You see my parents didn't want me to leave at all or at least stay here for two years and attend our local community college. There was a program there for students who wanted to become teachers. I didn't want to go to the only community college in town. My mom would be retiring after I graduated from high school. They were looking to save some money.

I wasn't going let it stress me out, I would listen to what they had to say, and then decide what I would do--after all the final decision would be left up to me.

Ding dong. "Who is it?" "It's Dame, girl open the door for yo new man " "See why you playing? I knew it was you." "Yeah right." "I told Shaun don't use his voice." "Shabria you are crazy." "What's up with you, baby girl?" "Hello Shaun." "Oh so now you like the ballers and the gangstas." "Whatever Shaun." "But I'm saying though, you ain't never tried to give a brother no play. What's up with that?"

"Why you in my business? It's time for you to leave Shaun, you can pick Shabria up on Sunday. Goodbye" "Meshay, why you do my brother like that?" "Because he hella nosey." "He jealous, you know." "But why?" "He really likes you." "Shabria, your brother is fine, but he ain't my type." "Girl what's to eat?" "I'll order a pizza." "Where's Mechelle?" "Upstairs."

So me, Shabria, and Mechelle ate pizza and watched videos. For once Mechelle was being nice, she even let Shabria braid her hair. I dozed off to sleep and awoke to execrating pain. I knew my cycle was coming but it seemed it was a few days early. I went to the bathroom, to look for some pads, but couldn't find any.

"Mechelle, Mechelle." "Huh." "Did you use all the pads?" "No." "Yes you did, that's why I asked mama to buy you your own stuff. Damn, I'm not fixing to walk all the way to the store, and I'm damn sure ain't getting on the bus." "Girl what's wrong with you?" "My cycle just started, and I'm out of pads."

I knew I was pushing it, but I had to drive to the store. I wasn't about to walk, I was in too much pain. So me, Mechelle, and Shabria went to the store. I was cramping so hard, I let Shabria drive. The only car keys left were the extra spare to the Mercedes. I told Mechelle she bet not tell. If she did, I would tell on her that Ms. Rosie came by to tell mama that she was being sassy and talking back again.

So we went to the store. We came straight back, luckily we had no problems. Shabria parked the car in the same spot. We chilled for the rest of the night. I hated having my bratty sister keep a secret. But sometimes desperate times cause for desperate measures, and what my parents didn't know wouldn't hurt them.

Summertime

Once my parents came back from Las Vegas, we sat down and discussed my options for college. We agreed that I would attend a business college for two years-- I chose Holmans. I would get my Associates Degree in Child Development. If I chose to stay, I would continue or I could move to Sacramento and attend Sacramento State to get my degree in Teaching.
They would also purchase me a car, or give me the Mercedes. I wanted my own car, and I wasn't into to luxury cars and felt the Mercedes would draw too much attention. My parents said we would go look for cars after graduation.

I had just gotten my license but my parents were still strict about me driving, especially their cars. That's why I couldn't dare tell them I let my best friend Shabria drive while they were in Las Vegas.

It was June 2nd, school was about to be out in two days, and summer was finally on its way. I would be a senior next year. Mechelle would be in the 8th grade. I was glad that I would be graduating by the time she entered high school.

I was turning 17 on September 26. I thought about asking my parents for a party, but decided to wait until I turned 18 instead. I was glad I would finally get a chance to work once I graduated high school. The City Parks and Recreation Department was accepting applications for Recreation Leaders. I was going to apply. Unlike my previous years of getting denied for Summer Youth Programs, this position had nothing to do with your parents' income.

I could have worked at the community center with my mom, but she said no because I needed a little bit more experience for the type of programs she was in charge of. So I would be working at a school. I would be working with the after-school program. I would be in charge of leading a group of about 15 kids in kindergarten to 6th grade.

RRRRRRing. "Hello." "Meshay, what are you doing?" "Nothing.". "Oh, guess what. My cousin Nikky is having a party for her 18th birthday and guess who her boyfriend is." "Who?" "Garren.". "Who is Garren?" "They call him G, and he is best friends with

Dame." "So." "Meshay, don't act like you still don't like the boy." "Shabria, I never said I liked him. I said I want to get to know him." "Girl, quit playing yourself, you know you sprung of Dame."

"Shabria, why you care? I thought he was no good for me?". "Mechelle, you are my best friend, we may not agree, but if you like him, then I'm going to help you talk to him. I just hope you know what you're getting into." "So when is the party?" "Tomorrow." "Tomorrow?" "Yeah." "Okay I'll try hard to convince my parents to let me spend the night." "Okay call me later." "I will."

"Mama can I spend the night at Shabria's house?" "Meshay, Shabria was just over here, so why is it that you want to go over there?" "Mama I never get to go over her house, and okay we are going over to her cousin's house for a slumber party." "Let me think about it." "Okay but it's tomorrow, but I was hoping I could go to Shabria's tonight." "Who is going to take you, I'm tired and you know your father is not going to drive you to that part of town." "I'll ask Shabria if her brother can pick me up".

I was surprised that my mom let me go over Shabria's house. She felt Shabria was left unsupervised too much. I explained to her that Shabria's mom had to work two jobs and just like us she was determined to make it out of the hood as well. Shabria was the middle child. Shaun was the oldest and Steven was 11, a year younger than Mechelle.

Shabria had lost her dad when she was five years old. He was giving a friend a ride one night and didn't realize the friend was actually going to rob somebody, so when the friend came running out of the house and demanded Shabria's dad to drive off, it was too late--the guy shot both of them. Shabria's mom was pregnant with Steven.

At the time, Shabria's dad had just got a real good job at the Army Base in the Bay Area. They were planning on moving to the Bay Area. This tragedy changed their lives forever. Shaun remembers more since he was older, and I think that's why he is so nonchalant about every thing. He probably doesn't feel like he should live life to the fullest.

Shabria handles it okay, and Steven wasn't even born. Their mom, Selena, is doing the best she can do.

She hasn't remarried, but she has a boyfriend, and of course neither of the kids like him. So I don't judge Shabria; she has been through a lot. She isn't like all of the rest of them ghetto broads, she hasn't had sex, and she doesn't even have a boyfriend.

A Party Ain't A Party Till I Walk In

My mom decided to let me stay the night at Shabria's house and attend what she thought was an all-girl slumber party. Since I knew Dame was going to be there, I had to look extra cute. I needed to pick the right outfit. I didn't want to wear a skirt since it was night; it was mid summer so jeans would have been too hot. So I decided to wear my blue capris with the red trim, a red top, and my red-wedged sandals that tied around my calves. This would be my first time I would be attending a house party. I had been to dances at school but I knew this wasn't going to be anything like a dance.

"Bout time you came, I was about to fall asleep." "Well I had to wait for Mr. Perfect to take a shower and get dressed. You got all your stuff?" "Yeah." "Bye, Mama, I'll be back on Sunday." "Bye Meshay, and be careful." "Hi Shaun." "Hey Meshay. You coming to hang out in the hood this weekend huh?" "What's that supposed to mean." "I'm not that bougie; I still know were I come from." "Chill girl, I'm just messing with you."

Shaun dropped me and Shabria off at their house. We stayed up most of the night talking about the party and what we was going to do, and what songs we were going to dance to. I told Shabria I was going to play it cool when Dame tried to holla. She was like what if he don't, I said he will, wait until he see me in my fit. I told Sharbria to twist my hair in the front, and I was going to flat iron the back. Shabria and I ended up going to bed around 12 midnight.

We arrived at the party at 8:00 pm--wasn't hardly anybody there but Shabria's cousin and some females I knew from my old neighborhood. There were a few guys there but nobody I was interested in. I decided to have a seat and chill; it seemed this was going to be an interesting night. Shabria and her cousins were dancing, but I wasn't ready to. I started to get up and walk over to the table where the punch was at and pour me something to drink.

As I was walking back to my seat, I saw Dame and about six of his friends coming through the patio door. I sat back down and acted like I didn't see him. A few of the guys started dancing with Shabria and her cousins. Shabria called me out to dance. As I was walking over to where Shabria was, Dame was coming towards me. "Hey Ms. Lady, watcha doing in my neck of the woods?" "You don't own this neighborhood, and for your info I'm from this side of town too." "Oh really, Ms. Lady. Okay so if you so down then how about get down with me?" "Excuse me?" "I mean let's dance Ms.Lady." "I guess so."

So that's how it was, me and Dame danced to three songs, and by the end of the night we had exchanged numbers. It went better than I expected. The next morning Shaun took me home. I was so tired I showered and went to sleep. When I woke up my mom had made dinner. I ate and cleaned up the kitchen. I was finishing up the dishes when Mechelle came in. "There's somebody on your phone." "Who told you to answer it?" Me, myself, and I." "Don't just walk in my room and pick up my phone." "I don't have to listen to you, I'm telling mama it's a boy on the phone too."

"Hello." "What up wit it." "Hey Dame. Nothing I was just cleaning up." "Oh Cinderella gotta do all the chores before she can go out and play?" "Naw it's not like that. So what are you doing?" "I'm just at my boy's house watching the game." "Oh that's cool."

"So when can I see you again?" "I don't know, I can't date until I'm 17." "Well how old is you now?" "I'm 16." "When will you be 17?" "In September." "Oh that's almost around the corner."

I talked to Dame for about an hour. I found out he lived with his uncle. His mom was in jail, and his dad was murdered when he was 12 years old. He told me about his trouble with the law--that he got caught selling marijuana. He did his time and now he wanted to change. He was looking for a job, and that's how he heard about my mom's program.

After talking to Dame, I didn't see him the same as every other guy--yeah he was a bad boy, but he did have some good in him. I guess that's what made me attracted to him. He looked all hard, you know like the player type, but once I got a chance to talk to him, I found out he wasn't too bad after all.

I like getting to know Dame. I knew I wouldn't be able to go anywhere with him, not just because I couldn't date until I was 17, but because of the fact of his background. I knew I wouldn't be able to convince my parents, especially my dad, but I wasn't going to let that stop me from still talking to him on the phone.

I knew I would see him every now and then, but not the way I wanted to. Eventually I would figure out a way to date him.

Class is in Session

It was August and summer was over. I enjoyed it all too well. I got a chance to hang out with Damien. Even though I wasn't allowed to date, I was still able to hang out with Shabria. So every chance I got, I let Dame know where we was at, if it was the movies, the mall, the park, even the library. He agreed to meet me. So that's how I found the way around dating him. Up to this point, I was never alone with Dame.

I knew I would be turning 17 in a month. This would be my last year in high school. Graduation would be in June, and I would start my new job in July at Lakeview Elementary School. I would get my car after graduation. My mom would be retiring in September. She said she wanted to stay long enough to see me get my foot in the door, and to let people know that I was her daughter.

I would start Holmans in the fall a few weeks before my birthday. I decided to get my A.A in Child Development. If I continued I would also get my B.A. I was looking forward to my new job and attending a business college. Most of my friends from school were going away. Although me and Shabria attended different high schools, we were still graduating the same year. But Shabria would be attending our local community college.

My first day of school was fun, I guess the fact I would be graduating this year made it all the better, or the fact that my dad let me drive his baby to school and keep it till lunch. Since this was my senior year, I was able to go off campus for lunch. On my lunch break, I took the car back to my dad. I was pulling up at the restaurant when I saw Dame's car. I walked in and saw him sitting at a table with two older guys.

"Hey, Daddy." "Hey baby." "You ready to go, cause I have to be back at school." "Okay baby, let me tell Rochelle I'll be right back." "Meshay, come here. what's up girl? Oh this is my uncle Frank and his best friend Mike." "Hi, nice to meet you." "Yo pops own this place?" "Yeah." "So why you ain't at school?" "I had to bring my dad his car--he let me drive it to school this morning."

"Meshay, come on." "Okay. Damien, I'll call you later." My dad drove me back to school and said he would pick me up later. It was 5th period and I was walking into my Earth and Plant Science class. As I was sitting there going over my project with Danielle, my mind kept wondering, thinking about Dame. "Meshay, Meshay." "Huh." "Pass me the book." "Oh I'm sorry Danielle, my mind is somewhere else." "Well I can see that." "Do you still want to go to the library this weekend to finish up the project?" "Yeah that's cool."

"Okay, class that's it for today." Mrs. Feldman dismissed us from class. I was glad this day was almost over. I knew the first day of school would be hard--so many assignments and senior projects. I was overwhelmed at first. Most of the projects that we had to do were in groups of two or more. Since my freshmen year, I hadn't made many friends. I really wasn't being anti social; it was just that I was one out of five Black kids that went here. I'm not saying I was prejudice but most of the White girls here were cheerleaders and very uppity, except Danielle--she was cool. So I was glad that she and I had the same classes, so working with her was going to be fun.

I never even looked twice at any of the guys in my school. I hadn't ever dated out of my race and hadn't planned on it either. There was a guy in my class, who was biracial, but he never even gave me a thought. I felt the same. The only other guy, who was Black, really didn't want to be, so we truly didn't have anything in common. I think this made me what to continue to date guys from my old neighborhood. I needed to feel a connection, and I wasn't trying to be so wrapped up in my new environment that I didn't recognize were I came from. Most girls my age was going through that same phase of falling for the wrong guy.

Birthday Girl

My birthday dinner was real nice--my parents took me, Shabria, and Danielle to an Italian restaurant. The food was great--I ordered lasagna and ravolies. We finished dinner by 9:00 pm, and I convinced my parents to drop me and my friends off at the bowling alley. Most of the teenagers hung out at the bowling alley on Fridays. My parents agreed and said that they would be back at 11:00 pm to get us.

I called Damien as soon as I got out the car and told him I was at the bowling alley. So me, Danielle, and Shabria got a lane and started bowling. As we were about to start another game, Damien and some of his friends walked in. As he was approaching me, I notice he had something behind his back. I was about to ask what it was when he handed me a white teddy bear with a red heart. "Happy Birthday." "Damien, you didn't have to buy me anything." "Yeah, I wanted to make my girl feel special." "I'm your girl?" "You want to be, right?" "I guess, I mean you know my parents would have a fit." "Well how bout we just keep this between us, for now." "Okay."

That's how Damien and I started going out on my 17th birthday. Even though I didn't let my parents know, Shabria and Danielle knew. The next morning me, Shabria, and Danielle went to the mall. I spent most of the money that was on the gift card that my parents gave me. Later on that night, me and my friends kicked it and watched movies. I enjoyed my 17th birthday and definitely would be looking forward to next year's 18th.

On Sunday morning, my mom made us breakfast, and that afternoon we took Shabria and Danielle home. I had to finish my homework, but decided to call Damien. "Hello. What are you doing?" Who's this?" "What?" "Hey, Meshay." "Oh, now it's just hey Meshay. "The other night I was your girl." "Baby, you are my girl." "Whatever, Damien. "Well I was just calling to say thank you for my teddy bear." "You're welcome, you know I got you. So when can I take you to the movies, can I get some alone time with you?" "Maybe, well see, when you start recognizing my voice."

I got off the phone with Damien and finished up my homework. The next morning for school I wasn't feeling too good so I stayed home. My mom said she would call in so she could sit at home with me since my dad wasn't at home. He usually doesn't go to Clovers until 10:00 am, but he was out of town purchasing a new stove for the restaurant and some stuff for the club as well. I told my mom, I would be fine. I went back to sleep and awoke to the phone ringing. "Hello." "Baby, what's wrong?" "I'm sick, why?" "I know, I heard your mom talking to somebody at the center." "Um, okay, I'll call you back Damien" "Wait, what's your address?" "No, you are not coming over." "Meshay, I just want to give you a hug, and make sure you're okay." "All right, it's 1112 East Denver Avenue."

I knew I was pushing it, letting Damien come over. I threw on some shorts and a t-shirt, and washed my face. I hurried downstairs when I heard the doorbell ring. "Who is it?" "It's Dame." I opened the door slightly. "Meshay, why you tripping?" "Cause I'm not suppose to have company, and my father could come home at any minute." "Come on baby, I'll just be here for 20 minutes." I let Damien come in, and I showed him around the house--he admired it and said I was lucky my parents moved me out the hood. He also thought I was lucky that my parents were still together.

Damien left, and I went back upstairs to my room. I was starting to fall in love with Damien, and I knew he had this control over me despite what I wanted or said--he could always convince me otherwise. This was my first relationship, although I didn't feel threatened by Damien, I actually liked the control, I felt he was older and very mature.

I didn't want to keep our relationship a secret, but I knew my parents, especially my dad, would have a fit if they knew. Over the next few weeks, I spent more time with Damien. We finally went out alone. He took me to the movies and out to eat. He even took me to a barbeque at one of his friend's house. I was so in love with Damien, but I didn't want to tell him.

By now Shabria had gotten her license, and Shaun bought her a car, so now it was easier for me to kick it with Damien. I now had better ways to come up with excuses. So one night I was with Damien, and we were going to get something eat. "Meshay, we been kicking it for a minute." "Yeah, I know, it's been two months." "I'm feeling you girl, and you know I love you." "What, are you for real?" "You seemed surprised." "I am." "So what, you don't love me?" "Yes, I love you Damien." "Well baby, I'm ready to take this to the next level." "Damien, are you asking me to have sex?" "Baby, I'm not trying to rush you, if you ain't ready." "I don't know, I never done it before."

I thought about what Damien wanted--I knew I wasn't ready--but I also knew that if I didn't have sex with Damien, he would have sex with some other female. I didn't want Damien to leave me, but I also didn't want to get pregnant. I wasn't on birth control. How I was going to ask my mom to put me on the pill, she would be wondering why. I sure couldn't tell her my boyfriend was ready for us to have sex.

Love Me or Leave Me

It only seemed like a few weeks, but actually it had been almost four months since I met Damien, and two out of the four we started going out. My senior dance was in a week, and I still hadn't been asked by anyone, nor did I want to. Me and Danielle had decided to go together, but now she says that she got asked by someone. Danielle said I could go with her and her date, but I didn't want to be the third wheel. I wanted to ask Shabria but I know she would be going to her senior dance. I wanted so badly to just ask my mom if I could go with Damien, but that would mean I would have to tell her and my dad that I had been seeing him secretly for four months.

I wasn't much interested in the dance being that this was only one of the events I had to look forward to my senior year. I was more interested in the fact that I was able to use my dad's car for the whole night and I didn't have to be home until 2:00 am. I was planning for me and Damien to be together. I knew he had been wanting to have sex, and I felt I was ready, and since it would be his birthday the night of my dance, I figured we would get a room. I would finally give him want he wanted. I was ready to prove to him that I loved him, and I wasn't about to have him leave me.

"Meshay, are you ready to go, the store closes in a few hours." "Okay, Mama, here I come." We got to the store, and it was crowded. I was having so much trouble picking out what color to wear. "Mama, what do you think about the red one?" "No, I don't like it." "Meshay, try the black one, black makes you look smaller." "Everybody is going to be wearing black. Mama, what about this one?" "Silver, Um I guess, try it on. Oh Meshay, that's pretty, we may have to get it altered." "Yeah, it's a little long."

After I picked out my dress, we went to the shoe store and to the cleaners to have my dressed altered. I was getting my hair and nails done. I was so excited. I wanted to by a new panty and bra set, but I didn't want to get one while I was with my mom. What I had in mind would be a little bit sexier than what I normally buy. I hadn't told Damien what I was planning, but I did let him know I would leave the dance early so I could give him his gift for his birthday.

It seemed like this night was dragging along. I was only staying until 10:00 pm. I wanted to have as much time as possible with Damien. I told him to meet me at Jays, which was one of our spots. I told him to come by himself, so we could have some time alone. Danielle and I took pictures--I figured at least I would do that. The dance was not as bad as I thought--I even danced with someone from my 3rd period class. It was 9:50 pm--I said goodbye to Danielle, and I left the dance.

I was so nervous the whole time on my way to meet Damien. I hadn't told Shabria or Danielle what I was planning. I knew both of them would talk me out of it. They wanted to remain virgins until there were married. I on the other hand wanted Damien to be my first. After all I felt in my heart, he may be the one I would marry.

I pulled up at Jays but didn't see Damien's car. I waited, and he pulled up about 20 minutes later. "Damn baby you look good." "Thank you. Oh here, I got you something." I reached in the back seat and gave Damien his gift. "Baby you got me a $100 dollar gift card." "Yeah, I know you like to be fitted." "That's what I'm talking bout. I'm hungry too, lets go in." "No, wait." "What you don't want to eat?" "No, not really. I was thinking, maybe we could get a room" "A room, as in hotel?" "Yeah, I wanted this night to be special. "I love you Damien, and I want to make you happy." "Meshay, I want you hella bad, but I don't want you to regret this." "I won't, I'm ready to be with you Dame."

I was ready as ever to have sex with Damien, and as I laid there ready for him to enter me, I was scared, and nervous. I tried to relax--Damien was patient, he kissed my neck, and my breast. He never once forced himself on me. Although it was painful, I tried to enjoy it, but yet this was so uncomfortable, I felt like my coochie was on fire, each thrust in and out. I wanted him to stop, but I just laid there, hoping he would be finish soon. I knew it was going to feel like this, but I think it had more to do with the fact Damien was well endowed, even though this was my first experience, I still knew Damien had a big penis.

"Baby, you okay." "Yeah, I'm just sore." "Come here. Girl, I love you for this. You didn't have to go through wit it. Don't trip, it gets better." "I guess." "Come on, let's take a shower."

I took a shower with Damien, and we got dressed. I headed home thinking I'm growing into womanhood. I may have only been 17, which for some was too young to be having sex, but what I felt for Damien was real. I mean, isn't your first love suppose to feel this way. I kept thinking, what Damien said, about the next time, it will be better. I knew I had to find some way of getting on the pill. "Oh, shit! I hope Damien used a condom."

Here We Go With The Drama

"Meshay." "Yes." "Go get your sister from the mall." "Mama, why you can't do it?" "Cause I'm tired." "Dang, why y'all let her go by herself anyways?" "Save that sassy attitude for somebody else." "Whatever." My parents think, I have to be responsible for Mechelle but they the ones who had her. I drove around the parking lot three times, and she wasn't there. I parked the car, and went to the south entrance so I could see if she was by the arcade. No Mechelle--see that's what I'm talking about.

I know damn well that is not my sister. I saw Mechelle sitting on some boy's lap that looked like he was about 18 years old. "What the hell are you doing?" "What, you ain't my mama?" "I know you better get your butt in the car." "Dang, Meshay, we just kicking it. Come on Cassandra." "Oh hell no, where she going?" "She needs a ride home, duh." "Where she live?" "By Shabria." "No Mechelle", "I'm not driving way over to the other side of town." "Please Meshay." "Alright, come on."

I took my bratty little sister's friend home. I noticed a familiar car, parked outside her house, and as I pulled up closer, sure enough it was Dame's car. Being that my nosey sister was in the car, I had to play it off. "That's a nice color car, is it your brother's car, Cassandra?" "Nope, that's Dame's car, he go wit my cousin, and they have a baby." "Oh, is that so?" "You know him?" "No not really. But my best friend live around the corner, and I seen that car before. I knew it belong to a dude though." "Well thanks for bringing me home. Bye Mechelle".

"She kind of grown, how old is she?" "15, and why?" "Don't you think you should hang out with people your age?" "She is my age; I will be 14 in a few months." "Whatever, brat." "You should stay out of people business, You act like you want her cousin's man, I know you know him, cause he be at mama's job, and I seen him, looking at you before."

I couldn't wait to get home, I was so mad, how could I not see it, and why didn't Shabria tell me Damien had a baby. We been together two months, and now I'm starting to get played, I can't believe this. Rrring, Rrring, Rrring "Hello." "Shabria, you supposed to be my best friend, and you couldn't even tell me Damien had a baby." "What are you tripping for Meshay? I don't know what you're talking about." "Shabria, don't lie to me, I don't need you to try and protect me, I can handle myself." "Meshay, what the hell is going on?"

I told Shabria how I took Mechelle's friend, Cassandra, home, who lived around the corner from her, and I saw Damien's car parked in front of their house, and Cassandra told me that the car belongs to her cousin's boyfriend, and that they had a baby together. Shabria told me that she knows Cassandra, and her cousin Tranay, but she didn't know the girl was pregnant, she's only 16, so what in the hell is Damien doing with her and he is 19. Shabria gave me the third degree, about being with him, and I should be careful, and don't start having sex with him, for I be next.

I couldn't tell Shabria, I already did. I wasn't ready to tell no one. What I needed to do was call Damien and find out what was going on. I don't know how to come at Damien; I didn't want to be accusing him without knowing for sure. "Hello." "Damien, we need to talk." "What's good, boo?" "I'm fixing get straight to the point. Are you cheating on me?". "What?" "Come on Dame, who is Tranay? Yeah you didn't think I was going to find out." "Man what is you talking bout Meshay?" "I seen your car parked at her house. I guess you was visiting yo baby." "First of all, what the hell you doing following me?, Don't be coming at me all crazy, Meshay, I ain't wit these games."

"Damien you need to be real with me, just answer the question." "Alright, the little broad was pregnant, she just had the baby. I went over there to see if he looked like me." "So you admit you messed with a 16 year-old." "Yeah, and you was 17 when I messed with you." "Well I'm supposed to be your girl." "Meshay, I messed with that girl way before I even met you." "So is the baby yours?" "Hell naw, that's the homies' baby, shit probably the whole hood. Man, Meshay, don't ever come at me with no he say she say shit. You ask me first, I ain't wit that gossiping. How you see my car anyways?" "I dropped some little girl off named Cassandra." "Oh I guess she said I was her cousin's man. You believed a 15 year old, man she a liar just like her cousin."

I didn't know how to feel or what to say about this Damien situation. I mean he did admit he messed with her, but he seen the baby and he doubt it's his. I don't know if I should believe him or not, I know I'm supposed to trust him, but he wasn't even trying to convince me, he was being more defensive and angry that I found out. If this is his baby, it's going to hurt, and I don't know if I can accept that he has a kid. I know he messed with Tranay before me, and we never really discussed our past. For me, Damien was my first boyfriend and sexual partner, so I really didn't have a past before him. If it is true, how come Shabria didn't even hear about it? I knew it would be some drama being with Damien. Just cause I'm no longer living in the hood, doesn't mean I'm blind to the fact what goes on. Damien wasn't no different from any other guy, and just because he claimed he loved me, still doesn't prove he was going to be faithful. The question was how much I was willing to put up with.

Girls Just Want To Have Fun

I couldn't stop thinking about this Damien and Tranay situation. Damien could possible have a baby by a 16 year old. I didn't want to keep doubting Damien, but he did admit to sleeping with this girl, and just because he feels the baby don't look like him doesn't mean it isn't his baby. I was glad that he was at least honest about the fact he messed with her way before he even met me, and that he isn't still messing with her.

I felt our relationship was different now, even though we still spent time together, and I continued to have sex with him. I was more cautious, and I found a way of getting birth control pills from my doctor without my mom being suspicious. Ever since I started my cycle at the age of 12. I have always had bad menstrual cramps and irregular periods. My mom said that it was normal because most of the women in my family went through it, and that is partially the reason me and Mechelle started our cycles so early.

So because of this, my doctor suggested I get on birth control which was what I told my mom. In actuality my last pap smear revealed I was sexually active, but even though I was under 18, my doctor didn't discuss anything with my mom unless she asked. She just advised me to take my birth control as prescribed, and to come in if I experience any symptoms that may be caused by contracting an STD.

"Hello." "Meshay, what are you doing?" "Nothing, just studying for our science test." "Ooh, sounds like fun. Hey you want to go to the movies this weekend?" "I'm sorry Danielle, but it's my sister's birthday. I promised my mom I would be nice and take my sister and her friends skating." "Wow, sounds cool." "Not really, my sister can be difficult." "Well maybe I should come and keep you company." "Are you sure you want to be around a bunch of bratty 14-year-olds?" "Come on Meshay, you make it seem like your sister is a demon child." "Almost." "Bye, Meshay, I'll talk to you later." "Bye, Danielle."

I decided since Danielle was coming, I would also ask Shabria to come and bring Steven. I wasn't really up to taking Mechelle and her friends skating, but I did make a promise to my mom, and at least I would have my friends to keep me company. I knew how it was being 14. When I was Mechelle's age, I did have my older cousins to look after me. So I felt I should start being more of a big sister to Mechelle. I tried even though it was hard, I don't know why my sister was such a brat, and why she got on my nerves. I guess in some way I was spoiled and didn't want to share the attention with another sibling.

"Come on Mechelle, we still have to pick up your friends." "Okay, dang I need to change my top." "Mama, we fixing to go." "Okay, you have money, Meshay?" "Yeah, I have some. Ooh, Mama did daddy put gas in your car?" "Richard, did you gas up my car, Meshay is leaving to take Mechelle skating?" "Yeah, baby you know I did. "Alright Mama, we're gone." "Bye Meshay." "Bye Mama, Bye Daddy." "Bye girls, y'all be careful."

I picked up Danielle, and we went to get Mechelle's friends. Shabria and Steven were going to meet us there. "Okay, Mechelle where are we going?" "By Shabria's house, remember." "Hold up, you didn't say Cassandra was coming." "Well, duh she is my friend." "Well who is Brandy?" "That's my other friend, but she is already waiting at Cassandra's house."

"Great, a bunch of young grown-ass brats." "Meshay, oh my gosh, I can't believe you just said that." "Okay, Danielle just wait, by the end of the night, you will see what I'm talking about."

We pull up at Cassandra's house, I waited for Mechelle to go inside and get her little friends. As I was sitting in the car talking to Danielle, my sister and her friends came out. As they were walking to the car, two women were following behind them. One was a little older, which I assumed was Cassandra's mom, and the other was holding a baby. As they approached the car I got out. "Hi, I'm Tina, Cassandra's mom". "I'm Meshay, Mechelle's sister." Oh, okay. "I just wanted to make sure Cassandra was leaving with Mechelle." "Yeah, I'm taking them skating tonight for Mechelle's birthday. I'll have them back at 9:00 pm." "Okay that's fine, nice to meet you." "You too." I figured the girl holding the baby was Tranay, and for some strange reason, I felt that they weren't really that interested in who was picking Cassandra up.

We got to the skating rink and Shabria and Steven were already there. Mechelle and her friends got their skates and went to the floor to skate. Me, Danielle, and Shabria got a table and sat down. "Shabria, I went to pick up Cassandra and guess who comes out the house?" "Who?" "Some lady name Tina, and Tranay." "Really?" "Yeah." "So, you seen what she look like." "She ain't all that, she look hella grown girl." "Yeah, she look way older than 16. I mean, she light skinned with good hair, if it's hers, and she got a shape." "Well yeah, she had a baby at 16, of course she going be more developed now." "Who are you guys talking about?". "Oh Danielle, let me feel you in." "Remember I told you that I think my boyfriend is cheating on me." "Yeah." "Okay, well the little girl Cassandra that we picked up-- well the girl with the baby is her cousin Tranay. That's the girl who Damien is supposed to have a baby with." Yes, drama, I know."

Don't Make Me Act A Fool

Michelle White

Part Two

I Swear to Tell the Whole Truth

"Hello." "Meshay, guess what." Shaun just bought a Lexus." "What?" Yeah right Shabria stop lying." "No I'm serious; I'm looking right at it. Do you want to go with us to the bowling alley this weekend?" "I don't know I guess." "You know there's a concert." "Who's going to be there?" "Taz, Tribe 3, and Mystic." "Really?" "Yes girl and Shaun said we can go with him." "Okay, I wanna go." "I'll call you Friday when we are on our way to get you."

I was excited about going with Shabria and Shaun this weekend. Finally we get to do something fun. Our town didn't have much for teenagers to do except the movies, the arcade, and the bowling alley. The bowling alley had the most excitement, since they remolded it, there was now more things to do. So every now and then there would be talent shows, concerts, and even fashion shows. It was nice to see our local talent. This was supposed to be my weekend to kick it with Dame, but too bad, I want to hang with Shabria.

I remembered I also had to help my mom out at the community center this weekend, for their annual health fair. I told her I would pass out the cookies and punch to the participants. So I would have to tell Shabria to drop me off after the concert. At least I would have fun on Friday, if not the whole weekend.

"Mama, is it okay if I go with Shabria on Friday to the bowling alley?" "Meshay, aren't you supposed to be helping me out this weekend?" "Mama, I know I'm not staying over Shabria's. I'll have her drop me back off at home." "You know you spend a lot of time socializing for a 17-year-old. Maybe it's time for us to have a talk." "Mama, I don't want the third degree." "Well just be honest with me, Meshay. Either you have this talk with me or your father." "Are you going to tell daddy what we talk about?" "That depends on what it is, and if I should." "Okay Mama, what do you want to know?"

"Who are you involved with?" "What do you mean?" "Is there something going on with you and Shabria's brother Shaun?" "No, Mama I don't like Shaun." "Well who do you like? I know you're talking to somebody. I see you rushing to your phone every time it rings, and you never want anyone to answer it. Ever since your birthday, you've been acting different. I hate to ask, but are you having sex? Meshay, don't lie to me, I'd rather you tell me the truth than make me a grandmother before I'm 45" "Okay, Mama I do like someone that you wouldn't approve of--it's Damien Mama." "You mean Damien Waters from my program? No, I don't like it, but you're almost 18, and if that's who you want to be with, then so be it. But don't be crying to me when you're pregnant and your heart is broken. I'm not trying to judge Damien, but I know his background, and he has a long way to go to prove himself." "So is it okay for me to go out with him?" "Don't ask my approval now after you have been doing it all this time. I should ground you until you graduate. But I'm going to let you make your own mistakes. "I know one thing you better stay on them birth control pills." "What, what pills?" "Oh Ms. Thang don't play innocent now? You better hope your daddy don't fly off the roof. I won't tell him you are sexually active, but I will let him know you have a boyfriend. Oh and best believe I will be talking to Damien."

I was in shock, how did my mom know all of this and why didn't she say something before. It kind of makes me scared and nervous. I wasn't expecting her reaction to be so cool and calm. Now I'm more worried about what she is going to say to Damien. I don't know if I should give him the heads up or not. Well I am kind of glad she wasn't tripping that hard about me going out with Damien. For the most part my mom has always been cool; my dad is the one who blows everything out of proportion. I do feel relieved that I finally had this talk with my mom.

I wonder why she thought it was Shaun. I guess since I have been spending a lot of time with Shabria, well that is saying I been with Shabria, but in actuality I have been kicking it with Dame. So now the truth is out, and my mom knows I like Damien and I have been seeing him. I just hope that baby by Tranay is not really his. Now that I have somewhat of an approval from my mom, I wouldn't want anything to ruin my chances of continue my relationship with Damien.

Even though I have been sneaking around all this time with Damien, I was feeling guilty. My mom was never really hard to talk to, it was the way she said things. Like how she kept saying I'm going to get pregnant. She always puts the negative in everything or suggests something bad is going to happen. I think that's her way of scaring me into reality. I guess she feels if I'm scared, I won't do it. Which, in some way, is true? I'm glad I finally told the truth, cause the truth will set you free. Now I feel better, I don't have to sneak; I just have to be careful and not get pregnant. Me and Damien haven't had sex in a while anyways, that's why we were supposed to kick it this weekend. Even though we have done it more than once now, I still didn't have a need for it. My hormones weren't out of control. I wasn't craving him, I really didn't get horny. I was just having sex with Damien to please him.

I'm Not the One to Judge

Shabria and Shaun picked me up, and I must admit Shaun's car was nice. He had rims and music already. I don't know how Shaun was able to afford all these cars, he just bought his Lexus, he bought Shabria a car, and he even got his mom a car. Shabria said Shaun was trying to straighten up and leave that hustling behind him, she said he even got a job. I guess he must be doing really well at his job to be affording all those cars.

"Shabria, don't get lost up in there, and don't be talking to no dudes either, I'ma be in front posted, hit me on the cell if something goes down." "Dang, Shaun, you doing too much, ain't nobody asked you to be a chaperon. Come on Meshay, he tripping."

Me and Shabria walked in the bowling alley; it was so packed. There were females and dudes everywhere; you could barely see the stage. So I knew it was going to be hard to see who was performing. Me and Shabria walked around for a minute. Even though it was winter, it was pretty warm in there. I wished I would have left my jacket in the car, cause I was starting to get hot.

I thought Damien might be here, but I didn't see his car. I told him that I wasn't able to kick it this weekend, and that I had to help my mom out. He knew I was going out with Shabria though, but I didn't tell him where we were going. I figured he wouldn't come anyway. Damien don't like to be around a whole lot of people, he say it's because he always getting into with somebody.

"Meshay, ain't that Tranay over there?" "Oh yeah, it look like her." "I should go over there and ask her who her baby is by." "What if she say Dame, you know you gonna be hella mad, and ready to fight." "And if she do, I'm act a fool all up in here, and she gonna get a beat down." "Meshay, quit tripping, and don't even mind that girl. If Damien say that ain't his baby, then don't you think you should believe him?" "Whatever, I just feel something ain't right with that situation. I mean he ain't even positive that it ain't his baby." "Well tell yo man, to take a blood test."

Shabria was right, if I wanted to know the truth, then I needed to convince Damien to get a blood test. If

Damien didn't get one then I would break up with him, because this is killing me I need to find out if that's his baby.

I focused my attention back on having fun and tried to keep my mind of Tranay. I wanted to just go over there and confront her, but I wasn't trying to be fighting some ghetto hoodrat over no dude. either Shabria was right, I needed to trust that Damien was telling the truth, and if he wasn't then I knew what I needed to do.

After about what seemed like 20 songs we danced to, I was tired, and I knew I had to get up early. So me and Shabria walked out the bowling alley to find Shaun so we could leave. We finally caught up with Shaun, and were getting ready to get in the car. Shabria said I could sit in the front, and I was like I don't want nobody to think me and Shaun is together. She was like, you know you wanna floss in the front seat, and I kinda did.

As I was getting in the front seat, I saw Damien walking towards me, and for some reason he didn't look happy. "What the fuck is you doing here?" "What, I told you I was going out with Shabria. Damien what is you trippin for?" "Man yo all in the next dude's car, why the fuck you in the front seat anyways?" "We just switched places for a minute until Shaun was ready to leave." I could tell Damien was drunk, his eyes were red, and I smelled weed on him, so I knew he was high also. I was hella scared the way he kept grabbing on me, I was afraid of what he would do next. "Damien can you please let my arm go?" "Hell naw, you coming with me." "I can't I already told you I gotta be somewhere tomorrow." "Man you fucking lying. Meshay if you get back in that car, we done." "What, why, I'm not even doing anything."

Shaun walked up as me and Damien was arguing. "Is there a problem?" "Not if you mind your fucking business patna." "Who the fuck you talking to?" "Dame I ain't even fixin play wit you ass, I know you betta back off and come correct for I fuck you up." "Well what's up then, you all over here wit my broad." "Dame you already know it ain't like that, so you need to just chill, and let Meshay get back in the car." "Hell naw, she ain't going know where wit yo ass."

I couldn't believe what was going on, Damien and Shaun was arguing and about to get in a fight.

Shabria was hella scared, and so was I. Everybody started crowding around the car waiting for something to go down. Then Shaun's patnas starting walking up and so did Dames. I didn't know what to do. I just told Shabria to calm Shaun down, and I would try to calm Damien down. I told them not to leave me. So I walked with Damien to cool him down, he was still going off on me. As we passed a group of females, all I heard was somebody say "Who the fuck is Tranay's baby daddy get into it with this time?"

I ignored what I just heard, and I told Dame to get in his car and leave, and I would call him later. He still was hella mad and said I bet not call him at all, and he went to grab me and snatched the hood off my jacket so hard he scratched my neck. I yelled out for him to stop grabbing on me. I jerked away from him, and walked off. I got in the car with Shabria and Shaun. My hair was a mess and I was starting to cry. Shaun looked over at me and asked if Dame hit me, I didn't know whether to respond, fearful of what he might say or do, and then Shabria said, "Meshay your neck is bleeding a little." I grabbed some tissue from out of my purse, and wiped my neck.

"Shabria, I'ma drop you off first." "We gotta take Meshay home." "I know, I'll take her, I gotta handle something, and I aint trying to back track. So it's easier for me to drop you off first." "I'm sorry you guys." "Meshay, it ain't your fault, Damien was drunk, he probably was guilty of something, that's why he was tripping with you. Girl don't let him upset you, I know you're hurt cause he was grabbing on you, but he wasn't fixing to hit you."

We dropped Shabria off at home, and we were on our way to my house. "Meshay, I need to stop by my house." "We just left your house." "Naw, I got my own place." "I'll just stay in the car." "No, you need to come in and get yourself together, I know you don't want yo moms to see you like that." "Do I look bad?" "No, but you look like you been in a fight. You ain't tripping is you?" "No I'm cool, after tonight you must really like me." "Why you say that?" "Cause you was about to fight my boyfriend, and ain't nothing ever happened between us."

That night I learned a lot about Shaun, I misjudged him. He was becoming a man. We talked about a lot of stuff, he explained to me that he ain't where he wants to be, and that he know he needs to stop hustling, but it brings in fast money and he doesn't want to see his mom struggle. That's why he made her quit her second job, and he went out and got a job. Shaun is into cars, so it is so fitting that he works at a car lot. He ain't no car salesman, but he works in the back and he said that's how he was able to get everybody a car.

Shawn said don't nobody even know he has his on spot, because he wants his mom's boyfriend to think he still lives at home. Shaun is afraid that once he leaves for good, Kevin, his mom's boyfriend might do something to her. Shaun thinks he hits her, and that's why he was all up in Damien's face tonight. He said he knows Damien has some violent tendencies and he wasn't about to stand there and watch him put his hands on me.

I felt more comfortable with Shaun, and was surprised when he told me how much he cared for me, and that I should leave Damien alone. He told me I could do better. I kind of understood what Shaun was saying. I mean I never thought me and Dame would get into it like this. I hope we work things out because I still love him. I told Shaun it was funny how we were sitting here talking because my mom swears up and down something is going on between us.

Shaun reached over and kissed me and said it should be. I didn't even stop him, I was enjoying it. I don't know, I guess it was the fact that he stood up for me tonight, but I felt something when Shaun was kissing me, and I didn't want it to stop. I wasn't even thinking about Damien at that moment.

Quiet As It's Kept

It was way past my curfew, and I knew my mom would be up. This was the first time I broke my curfew which was at 11:00pm, and I was almost two hours late. If it hadn't been for Shaun, convincing me to get my self together before I came home, I don't know what my parents reaction would have been if they were to know what just went down with Damien. Especially after me and mom just had a talk, and she somewhat agreed to let me keep seeing Damien. I couldn't imagine telling her he got drunk and was acting a fool.

I slowly crept up the stairs and as I was going into my room, my mom came out of hers. "Meshay, what in the hell is the matter with you?" "Mama I'm so sorry, really I didn't try and break curfew on purpose." "You should have called; you're starting to get a little bit besides yourself. I should really ground you for this, I just started to put a little bit more trust in you, and look you can't even keep curfew.". "Mama, I know, but the bowling alley was so packed, we had trouble getting out of the parking lot."

"I got a call from Officer Smith. He told me what happened, and apparently he saw you." "Huh, oh he did. Mama it wasn't my fault honestly." "I know. He said the concert got out of control, and by the time he could see what was going on the crowd disbursed. He said he was trying to make sure you were okay, but you must have already been gone, but he did say he saw you when you first got to the bowling alley".

It honestly slipped my mind--my mom's coworkers were working at the event. I would have been so embarrassed if I was to be seen as the one involved in a conflict. I was so scared; I thought my mom was going to say Officer Smith saw me and Damien arguing. You know this was pure luck; something more serious could have resulted from this. I do need to be more careful.

I'm starting to think that this relationship with Damien is too much to handle. I can't afford to cause any embarrassment to my parents. I need to tell Damien if he can't control his behavior then it's over between me and him. Shoot it might be over already, since Damien was still tripping that I left with Shabria and Shaun anyways.

I tried to get as much sleep as possible before it was time for me to wake up, and it seemed like as soon as I closed my eyes, it was already time to get up. I barely could sleep; all I could think about was the way Shaun and Damien got into it. I was scared because, in the back of my mind I remember Shaun saying that him and Damien was about to be enemies now. I even had a dream that Damien shot Shaun.

I have never seen Shaun get so mad, he never seemed like the gangster type, but after last night I know he ain't to be messed with. As far as Damien goes, I know his background, and he wasn't afraid to step to Shaun either, so I'm dealing with two dudes who ain't fearful of nothing, and they both have feelings for me. That's a deadly combination. I just hope this whole thing blows over. I pray nothing happens to either one of them.

I was so tired at the event, but I managed to keep it together. There was a pretty decent turn out. A lot of community resources were available. There were games and jump houses for the kids. They even had face painting and a clown. My mom was so involved; she made sure everything was kept in order. She even had me running back and forth to the store to make sure we didn't run out of cookies and punch.

My dad even came by and brought Mechelle. I called to see if Shabria wanted to bring Steven but she said she couldn't come out, and she would explain to me later. I was kind of shocked, and I hope she didn't blame me for what happened last night. I thought everything was cool, she didn't seem mad, and even Shaun wasn't tripping. They both said it wasn't my fault, so I don't know what's up now, but I couldn't wait to talk to Shabria later. I wasn't about to choose my boyfriend over my best friend.

Things started to wind down, and we were finishing up. My mom told me to go home with my dad and Mechelle. She said she was going to put some things away, and she needed to have a quick meeting with her staff. So I was like okay, I was ready to go anyway. I wanted to take a long bath and go to bed.

Once I got home, Shabria called me. "Meshay what are you doing?" "Nothing, just got home. What's going on with you, why you didn't want to come to the event?" "Shaun said he thought it would be a good idea if I stayed home." "Why he doesn't want me around you?" "No, he just thinks that Damien is still tripping. He didn't know if you and he were back together already or not." "I haven't even talked to Dame, so I don't know where we stand."

"Well he didn't know if Dame would be tripping with me too, since I am Shaun's sister." "Dang, Shabria, Shaun really thinks Dame is going to trip that bad?" "Apparently Dame is known for keeping shit going, he don't even be trying to resolve it." "Man, I hope not, but shoot I can't put anything past him, I'm finding out different things every day and it seems I really don't know what he is capable of."

I couldn't believe what I was hearing. I was starting to think Damien's lifestyle wasn't what I was looking for. I believed he was trying to change, but now I don't think so. I never wanted to judge Damien, and I thought people could change. I guess I wanted to see the good in Damien, and overlooked the violent tendencies, and the things he was capable of doing.

Like for one, the lying and the deceit. I was willing to accept Damien's behavior thinking he would change and I tried to give him a chance, but then I turned around and judged Shaun, and here he was actually making a change. Shaun was more of a man and Damien wasn't ready to fully become one.

Why You Wanna Act Like That

I called Damien. I couldn't let another day go by without us talking about our relationship if we still even had one. I thought Damien had cooled down and would be ready to talk, but he wasn't. He accused me of sleeping with Shaun, and that I chose the next dude over him. He said I disrespected him in front of his patnas, and that I was acting like a little tramp. I was so mad at him, I told him it's over, and that he could go and be with his baby mama, and I hung up in his face.

I felt like crying, but I knew I needed to just forget about Damien, and that I shouldn't let myself get upset over a relationship I knew was doomed from the start. Despite what everyone was telling me, I thought Damien was the one for me. I thought I would be the one he would change for. Even though I broke up with Damien, it wasn't going to be that easy to get over him, I still loved him, and I hoped that he would stop tripping, and quit acting like I was the one at fault.

I loved the relationship for the most part, but what I couldn't handle was the way Damien had been tripping lately, and I knew it had something to do with him possibly having a baby with Tranay, cause it seemed like ever since I confronted Damien he changed. I wanted so much to believe in him, but I overlooked the reality of the situation. I knew I wasn't going to be able to continue the relationship with Damien, our lifestyles were too different. The whole beginning of our relationship I was sneaking around to be with him, and when my mom did finally approve she wasn't that thrilled about me even seeing him.

I would always love Damien, but I didn't want to be so involved in him that I would lose a part of me. I was only 17 and I wasn't ready to be so emotionally involved. I already had to deal with the fact I was no longer a virgin, and I had been in a sexual relationship even before I was 18 years old. I didn't even think twice about waiting until I was older or even waiting to get married for that matter.

I made a choice to have sex with a person I knew deep down inside I wouldn't never be with for the rest of my life. I don't know how I was so blinded by Damien; I knew it had a lot to do with trying to fit in, and to feel like I belonged. I hadn't had that many guys asking me out, no one was my type. I was attracted to the bad boys; I figured they wouldn't be that way all their life, so when Damien showed an interest I was flattered.

My relationship wasn't all that bad; it just wasn't the right one to be in at this age. Well I learned my lesson, and now it's time for me to move on. As to if I can and if I will I don't know, I'm so confused I just want to take a break for a minute, and maybe me and Damien will work things out.

"Hello, can I speak to Meshay?" "This is her, who is this?" "Shaun." "Hey, what's up?" "I wanted to call and see if you were okay." "Yeah I'm cool." "You no I wasn't trying to be funny and break up you and Shabria's friendship." "Yeah, I know you were just looking out for your sister." "Okay, well I'm let you go, you sound like you don't feel good." "Yeah I guess you can say that, but thanks for calling Shaun."

Um, Shaun is really sweet; you would never have known that he was so kind and considerate. I wondered why he was so concerned about me and Shabria's friendship. I guess he figure we have been friends for so long, why would we let anyone come between that. I have known people to break up friendships over guys. I wouldn't ever do that, no matter how much I loved and cared for a guy. I would never lose my friendship with Shabria or Danielle. I would never choose my relationship over my parents either. I may have been sneaky and was wrong for seeing Damien, but I knew eventually if my parents were that strong against it, I would have to choose, and I knew I would make the right decision. I could be difficult at times, and go against my parents, but eventually I learned my lessons before it was too late. I just had to test the waters like most teenagers.

Can We Talk for a Minute?

I'm really getting fed up with Damien, he keeps calling, and I'm steady telling him we're done. Too much has gone on these past couple of weeks, and his behavior is worse. One minute he says he loves me, then the next he accuses me of being with somebody. I told Damien if he stopped calling me, and let me breathe for a minute that I would agree to talk to him, and maybe try and work things out. I just needed some space.

I went over Shabria's house so I could get my mind off my messed up relationship. As I was sitting in Shabria's room, Kevin, Selena's boyfriend walked in and told Shabria to do the dishes before her mom came home. "I can't stand him," Shabria said as she walked in the kitchen. I heard a glass break, so I ran into the kitchen, and I saw Kevin slap Shabria. I stood there and asked Shabria did she want me to call Shaun, she was like no it's okay Meshay, just go back in the room.

I went back in the room, and a few minutes later Shabria came in crying. "Meshay, come on let's go."

"Why, where?" "Anywhere, but here." So me and Shabria left. I told her to let me drive, cause she is too upset right now. I knew something more than Kevin just slapping her was going on. "Shabria, what's wrong?" "I'm tired of him, he thinks he's the man of the house. He ain't my daddy, and I'm tired of him hitting me." "Tell your mom or at least Shaun." "I cant, you know how Shaun is, I don't want my brother doing time for his stupid ass." "Man, I'm sorry you dealing with this." "I tried telling my mom, but she ain't trying to here it."

"You want to stay at my house tonight?" "No I don't want to leave Steven by himself. I'll just wait till my mom gets there, then I'll go home." "Dang Shabria, I thought me dealing wit Damien's crazy ass was bad" "I know girl, I can't wait till I graduate, I'm moving out." "Shabria, you should really tell Shaun, you know he will make a way for you and Steven to not have to deal with this." "I will, I'm just going to see if he stops first."

I was so worried about Shabria, I knew Shaun had his on apartment and that I should tell him so he could take care of Steven and Shabria, but Shabria was right, Shaun would kill Kevin if he found out. I didn't know what else to do, but pray that Kevin keep his hands off of her.

Thinking about what Shabria was going through, just made me think about Damien. I could have been the one getting slapped around--I mean Damien had the same violent tendencies. I knew I needed to go ahead and talk to him, and if we was done then so be it, and if I decided to work things out, then Damien was going to have to changes his ways.

Damien convinced me to meet him at Jays. I didn't want to confuse him and have him thinking we were getting back together. He said he knows things are pretty bad between us; he just wanted to talk without all the arguing and fighting. When I got to Jays, Damien was already sitting at a table. I walked over to him and sat down, he handed me a letter and told me to read it later.

"Meshay, I know I been acting crazy lately. Baby, I don't know what it is, I just know when I drink, I get crazy, I don't realize I'm tripping until its too late." "So why drink Damien, if you can't handle your liquor?" "I don't know, shit everybody be drinking." "You don't have to drink, 'cause all your friends do it."

"I like getting high and drinking wit my patna's." "Well I guess we don't need to be together then." "Meshay, if I promise to slow down, and not get out of line with you, can we get back together?" "Damien I don't know right now, you know I been going against my parents for you, and now you and Shaun got beef, this is a lot to deal with." "Baby I know but, I need you right now, you the only positive thing in my life. I ain't got nobody but you."

I wanted to believe Damien, maybe I was all he had. I know he has an uncle, but he don't have his biological parent raising him. I started to think what if his behavior was from not having his parents around. If so, then I couldn't just turn my back on him, ain't no telling what another rejection could do to him. So I decided to work things out with Damien only if he agreed to slow down on the drinking.

I also told him that he needed to change his behavior, so that he could meet my parents. If we were going to be together again, then he had to meet my dad. Damien was cool with meeting my parents; he said he was actually kind of glad I wanted him too. He said just cause he is from the hood that doesn't mean he didn't deserve to be treated like anybody else.

I never thought that maybe me always expecting Damien to be a certain way, could have played a part on his behavior. I mean if people are always thinking less of you, what makes you want to think any better of yourself. If I loved him that much, I should have accepted him completely--flaws and all. Thinking he was going to change over night because I was tired of him wasn't going to work, I had to be patient enough to know that for some guys like Damien, they probably ain't-- never seen how a real man is supposed to act.

Finally We Agree

"Dear Meshay, I know I have been acting fucked up lately. I'm not use to dealing with a girl like you. I'm use to females who ain't as outspoken as you. Meshay, you have a lot going for yourself to be so young, I mean your life is already planned out for you. You lucky you got parents that actually care about you. I know you ain't use to me, and my lifestyle, and I just been dealing wit so much, I'm not going to lie to you, yeah it's a possibility that Tranay's baby could be mines. I asked her for a paternity test, but she keep playing games. Meshay I'm just asking for a second chance, just let me be the man that I can be, and not what you want me to be.

I understood where Damien was coming from, and I decided to give him another chance. I was hurt by the fact that he may have a baby, but at least he was honest. I was starting to be more understanding to the way Damien was feeling. I loved him, and I wanted to work things out, it's just I started to think he would never be able to change. Damien was right I was lucky to have moved out of the hood, and because of this I thought that everyone who wanted to could have that opportunity as well.

What I didn't realize was it wasn't that easy for everyone, like with Shabria and her family, they tried but a tragedy happened and her father was killed. Even though Shabria's mom Selena is working, and has a man in the house, the situation still isn't any better, cause Kevin is not hardly a man, or a father figure for that matter. Selena is probably so blinded by the fact that she lost a husband, she is settling for what she thinks she needs in her life, another man.

It's a shame that Shabria and Steven have to suffer. I couldn't imagine going through that. I was glad my parents were still together, and that nothing has happened so far. I guess I wasn't really showing that I was truly thankful to my parents. I know it seemed that they never understood me, but I did have the freedom of making my own choices, and I did get to hang out and spend time with my friends, even when my parents really didn't want me to hang around my old neighborhood.

I decided to sit down and talk to my parents, about Damien. I wanted them to see I was serious about being with him. I needed to find some common ground with this situation, I wanted to be able to let my parents know I did have a boyfriend, and they needed to accept him, whether they like him or not.

"So Meshay, you want us to meet Damien?" "Yes Mama, I do." "Who is this boy, some thug huh?" "Daddy come on, don't be like that, Damien is cool." "Richard, the boy does have a background, but Meshay is right, stop judging people." "Well, I guess I do need to see what he's all about." "Thank you daddy. So can he come for Christmas dinner?" "Meshay, you know we're having the whole family here." "Mama, why can't he come, it's the holidays, dang." "Oh, alright I guess that would be best."

Finally we agreed on something. Damien would spend Christmas with us, and he would get a chance to meet my entire family. I was so excited, but now I was nervous not only did I have to worry about my parent's opinion, but the opinion of the rest of the family.

I told Damien I thought Christmas was the perfect time for him to meet my parents, well only my dad was the one who actually needed to meet him. Damien was fine with that, and he asked could he bring his uncle along, he wanted to show my parents that he did have a relative who was trying to raise him up right.

So that's how it was agreed upon to introduce my parents to Damien. I was coming to realize that I needed to start working with my parents instead of always against them. I knew I couldn't force them to like Damien, but at least they could be cordial in his presence. I just hoped my dad didn't embarrass me, and my mom didn't interrogate Damien, after all she does work for the police.

"What do you want Mechelle?" "Mama said can you take me to the library." "No I'm busy." "I need to get a book for my project." "Doesn't your school have a library, get one from there." "You're mean, I can't stand you." "My thoughts exactly." I had better things to do than take my bratty sister to the library. I'm pretty sure she's got plenty of books to work with. She just thinks I have to do what ever my mom says.

Normally I do, but not when it comes to her. I knew I wouldn't hear the last of it, so I may as well get up and take her. "Come on Mechelle, I'll take you, don't think we're staying all day either." "Mama said you can take me to the mall too." "For what?" "A gift exchange for one of my classmates." "Great, another Saturday spent with you." "You don't have to stay, just drop me off." "Yeah, right."

I browsed around the mall and got an idea of what to get Danielle and Shabria for Christmas. I also was looking for something to get Damien. I was planning on spending less than what I did for his birthday. I loved him, but I wasn't giving him another $100 gift card. My allowance was only $300 dollars a month, and I wasn't going to be left broke, I wanted to buy presents for everybody else, including myself.

This Is Who I am

"Meshay, you need to finish that macaroni and cheese." "Mama, I know." "Well baby I want everything done by 2:00 pm." "Mama you know mostly everybody going to be late." "Well, I don't care if they are, I still like to have this food done." "Why can't Mechelle help?" "Meshay don't start that, she did help; she peeled a few potatoes, and cut up some onions." "That's it?" "Well that's better than what she usually does and Meshay you need to be dressed on time please, you know how you get at the last minute."

I was so tired; I had been up since early this morning helping my mom cook. I still had to comb my hair and get dressed. I wanted to look cute, but still be comfortable. I wanted Damien to see me looking extra beautiful. As usual, I always have trouble finding something to wear, and I should have thought about this last night. I wasn't trying to be all dressed up, so I definitely wasn't wearing a dress.

I decided to take a chance and wear my cream sweater, some jeans, and my cream boots. I knew before the day was up I probably would have to change my sweater, being that I still would be in and out of the kitchen, helping prepare and serve our numerous relatives.

Ding Dong. "I'll get it. Hi Auntie, Brenda, Hi Uncle Raymond." "Hey, Meshay baby, where's your momma?" "In the kitchen." "You guys can put your coats in the guest room. Tanya and Aisha, you guys want something to drink?" "No, we're fine."

After about ten doorbell rings, it seemed most of my relatives had arrived for our Christmas dinner. I still was waiting on one more person, hoping that he would show up. "Meshay, who is this boyfriend of yours?" "I knew my nosey cousins couldn't wait to 20 question me about Damien. "Y'all get to meet him, dang." "Well I wanna know is he fine?"

I was helping my mom set all the food out so we could eat, then all of sudden I heard a bunch of hellos, and I heard my Uncle Allen ask was that a long lost relative of ours. I knew Damien must have been who he was talking about, so I tried to hurry up and rush into the living room before they said something embarrassing.

"Everybody, this is my boyfriend Damien, and his uncle Frank, and his wife Stacy." "Hi, nice to meet everyone." "Mama, Daddy this is Damien." "Hi, Damien." "Merry Christmas, Mr. and Mrs. Lewis."

Once Damien was introduced, everyone wanted to know his whole life story. My uncle Allen, him being the oldest relative, swore up and down he knew Damien. I had to constantly remind him, that he was not related to the Johnsons. Damien's' uncle Frank did happen to know some of my uncles, and his wife Stacy went to school with my cousin, Rochelle.

"Baby, yo uncle is crazy." "Don't mind him, he's drunk. Are you having fun?" "Yeah, I'm cool. I have a present for you." "I got you a little something too."

After we ate dinner, we all sat in the den and watched movies. I decided to go outside to get some alone time with Damien. Well here come my cousins Shawna, Kyla, and Aaron, they all suggested we walk to the park to get away from the adults. I was like I'm not walking its cold. So Damien was like let's drive. My cousin Aaron asked if the mustang parked in front was Damien's, and Damien was like yeah that's mines. So we all got into Damien's car and left. We were supposed to be going to the park, but here we go with the detours. Shawna was like let's go to the liquor store, and of course everybody agreed except me.

We ended up getting some alcohol and of course my cousins are pot heads too. I was hoping Damien would be trying to make a good impression, but no, he had to voluntary offer some weed to my cousins. I was like I'm not drinking or smoking with y'all. Everybody told me I was being a party pooper, and that I never like to have fun, even Damien said I act too high and mighty sometimes.

The more I tried to fight it, they wasn't even trying to her me. I was like I'm not like you guys, I'm not into drinking or smoking weed. So just accept me for me. My cousin Shawna was like Meshay quit preaching to us. So I sat back and let them continue getting high. I couldn't help it if this is who I am; I never have gotten high or even had a drink of alcohol.

"You guys need to spray some cologne or perfume." "Meshay, we know how to get rid of the weed smell." "Okay, we do have to go back to the house." "Baby it's cool, we ain't even that high."

"Whatever, let's just get back please." So me, Damien, and my cousins went back to the house. They all had fun while I was uncomfortable and probably had a contact buzz from just sitting in the car with them.

So I decided to go upstairs and change my sweater, fearful of having the smell of weed in my clothes. My cousins wasn't even tripping, they were loving Damien. Aaron was like he hella cool. I was glad that everything was going smoothly, even if my cousins and my boyfriend got high and drunk together. Things started to wine down at the house, everybody was starting to leave. So we started to say our goodbyes, and people were packing up plates to take home.

As I was letting relatives out the door, I saw that Damien's uncle Frank and his wife had left already, so I was wondering where he was; I knew he wouldn't leave without saying goodbye. I walked in the kitchen to see if maybe he was getting a plate to take home, but nobody was in the kitchen but Mechelle.

So I walked in the living room and my parents and Damien were in there talking. "Ms. Thang, have a seat. "Yeah we were just talking to Damien about your relationship. I let him know we thought you were a bit too young to be this seriously involved. Meshay you are about to be 18, so you will be an adult." "Damien how long have you been dating my daughter?"

I wasn't ready for my dad to ask Damien that question, neither was I ready for Damien to respond? "Sir, I met Meshay this summer at the mall. I did like her and wanted to get to know her, but she did tell me she couldn't really date until she was 17." "Um, I see, so technically you have being knowing my daughter for about six months now?"

Damien was trying to be as honest as possible with my parents without jeopardizing our relationship. My parents seemed a little bit more comfortable once they saw how Damien wasn't trying to deny our relationship. He even was honest about his trouble with the law. He explained to my parents the circumstances in which he grew up in, and this may have contributed to his behavior. I think my parents were starting to accept our relationship for the most part. I was glad that I got a chance to invite Damien over to meet my family. This was a nice Christmas, I don't know if my parents were just being nice because of the holidays, or were they truly going to let me continue seeing Damien.

Roses Are Red

I love most every holiday, but for some reason Christmas and Valentines Day is so special to me. I don't know if it's the color red, or the fact that people go out of their way to show their love on these two occasions. I was finally enjoying my relationship with Damien, and ever since Christmas it seemed like we were getting closer. My parents were no longer on my back, and I think they even started to like Damien.

I hadn't spent much time with Danielle or Shabria, so this was going to be an all-girls weekend. I decided I would pay for me and my friends to get our nails and feet done. We were going to spend the whole day at the mall and then go out to eat and maybe a movie. I promised them I wouldn't make any plans with Damien.

"Meshay, we're so glad that you fit us into your busy schedule." "Okay Danielle, I know I haven't made much time for you guys lately." "Yeah, Meshay, we were starting to think you no longer needed friends, since you have a man." "Shabria, I told you I would never choose Damien over you or Danielle." "Um, hum, if you say so." "So what have you guys been doing?" "Well since you have been in love me and Shabria have been hanging out." "Yep, me and Danielle have a lot in common." "I never thought that you guys wouldn't get along without me." "Well we just been going to the movies and out to eat." "Oh that's cool, I'm glad."

"Yeah Danielle is becoming part of the family." "What's that suppose to mean, Shabria?" "Oh, well Shaun and Danielle are talking." "What?" "Meshay, you're not mad are you?" "Yes, I mean no, but when did this happen?" "We only been talking for a few weeks. I been hanging out with Shabria and I thought Shaun was fine." "Danielle, I figured you would be into black guys." "Meshay, you don't have to say it like that, just because I'm White and my best friend is Black doesn't automatically make me want to date Black guys. I don't look at color I look at the person." "I know Danielle, I didn't mean to offend you." "Shaun is sweet, and I misjudged him in the past." "Yeah he told me he had feelings for you, but nothing ever happened between you guys."

"Well I hope you're happy, and I shouldn't be the only one with a boyfriend." "We're not officially a couple, so theres--only two of us at this table who is in a relationships." "Huh, Shabria?" "What, Danielle, I was going to tell her later." "Tell me what?" "I met this dude from out of state; he just moved here, his name is Carlos." "Is he Black?" "Yes, Meshay, why?" "Cause what kind of name is Carlos for a Black guy?"

"Well we met at the bowling alley one night, and we been talking ever since." "Dang, it seems like you guys just moved on with your lives."

"Meshay, that's what we're supposed to do, don't be mad because we didn't wait for your approval." "I'm not I just feel left out." "And so do we." "No I'm glad that you guys found someone to be with, 'cause I love Damien and I want my friends to be happy and be with someone that makes them happy." "So Meshay what are you and Damien doing for Valentines Day?" "She probably planning on taking their relationship to the next level." "Meshay are you planning on having sex with Damien?"

"You guys I already did." "Oh my gosh, Meshay." "I know I wanted to tell you guys, but I knew you would try and talk me out of it."

"So You been whining over him possibly having a baby with somebody else, but yet you damn near bout to give him one." "I know Shabria, but we have been careful, and I'm on the pill. I love Damien and I know he loves me, even my parents are letting me continue to date him." "Meshay, just be careful, you have so much to look forward to, just don't make any sudden plans, and keep your options open, Damien may be your first serious relationship, but he may not be your last."

I listened to what Danielle and Shabria had to say. I was so surprised to find out that my friends were no longer single, that they in fact were dating. Was I so wrapped up in Damien that I neglected my relationship with my two best friends--my only two at that. I was glad that Shabria and Danielle had gotten closer, but a part of me was jealous that they had, and that Danielle was into Shaun.

I knew eventually Shaun would find somebody, but I never thought it would be someone I knew; I guess I thought he would chase me forever. Well I can't have everything my way, and I'm in love with Damien so why does it even bother me that Shaun and Danielle are talking. I'm not going to let it though, because I truly think Danielle really likes him, and I would be selfish to come between them. I should have taken the opportunity to be with Shaun when I had it.

"Meshay, what's wrong?" "Nothing". "What you don't like my food?" "Dame it's good." "Oh, well you just were sitting there." "I'm not hungry." "Man what is it, I hope you ain't about to ruin are first Valentines Day wit some gossip." "Damien, I just got a lot on my mind." "Damn girl, what you pregnant?" "No, why would you think that." "Cause either that or something's up. Baby whatever it is don't let it stress you out. Here go into my room, and lay down and I'll bring you my famous chocolate sundae, since you don't want to eat my cooking."

I wish I was a little bit more in the mood, especially being this was me and Damien's first Valentines Day, but I couldn't stop thinking about Shabria and her new boyfriend, and Danielle and Shaun; wondering how they were spending their Valentines Day. Now that we all were in relationships, would we

Danielle tomorrow at the library." "What was so important, that you had to use my car right after school?" "Oh, I had to go the museum for an observation for my science class" "Well next time, you need to make appointments around my schedule; you know I like to get off early on Fridays." "I know mama, it slipped my mind, and I have to turn the paper in on Monday."

I dosed back off and slept the rest of the night; thinking my mind would be at ease once I got some rest but it wasn't. I couldn't let it distract me; it's bad enough I have been un-focused. This was my senior year, I wasn't about to become a drop out, so I had to continue on the right path. If that meant dealing with being pregnant, I still was determined to graduate on time.

"Hey, Danielle," "Hi Meshay, you look tired." "I am, but it's cool I'll be alright." "Okay I found a topic, what do you think about teen pregnancy?" "No, let's find another one." "But, Meshay, that's such a common topic." "Exactly, I don't want to do what's common."

What I really wanted to tell Danielle was I don't want to be writing a paper about myself. So we decided tomorrow." "No this is really important, and plus I don't feel good." "Alright then I'm a hang with my boys, don't be calling me tripping either." "Whatever, do what you want, Dame, bye."

At this point I didn't care who or what he was doing. I was too worried about my situation. A part of me was mad at Damien, he was the one always wanting to not use a condom. I know I should be more careful, but I was, I just messed up this one time. Shoot I'm trying my damnest to please him. I feel like crap, I got a bad ass stomachache. All I can do is lay here, my doctor said she won't have my results until Monday. I knew I should have skipped school and went to the doctor but, I wasn't trying to have any unexplained absences though, and I sure couldn't tell my mom I needed to go to the doctor. I wasn't even thinking; I forgot it was Friday and the lab closed early.

"Meshay, Meshay." "What?" "Mama calling you." "Um, alright get out my room." I couldn't hardly get out of bed, I was so drained. I slept through dinner; damn it was already 9:00 pm. "Meshay, didn't you hear me calling you?" "I was asleep." "I thought you had to finish your research paper." "I do, I'm meeting up with skipping your pills Meshay?" "I didn't--wasn't trying too, I just noticed I never got them refilled." "Um, well since you did come in after hours, I won't have the results from your test until Monday, the lab is closed." "Can I take a home pregnancy test?" "Those are not a 100% accurate, so I don't advise it. How many times have you had unprotected sex?" "I think maybe three times." "Are you having multiple sex partners?" "No, I have a steady boyfriend." "Well in the meantime, please be careful, and there's no need to start your birth control pills again until we know the results."

This is the worse day of my life. I know I'm pregnant. Things were going way too smooth. I should have known something was bound to happen. Everything can't be peaches and cream all the time. I don't know what to do, if I tell my mom I might be pregnant, she is going to have a fit. I couldn't even imagine the response of my dad. I know Shabria is going to let me have it. I really don't know what to do. All I can do is wait.

"Hello." "Damien, I don't want to go to the movies." "Why, what's wrong?" "Nothing, I just have a research paper to do." "Meshay you can do it

Patiently Waiting

I wasn't feeling well these last couple of days. I knew something was wrong, but I didn't want to think I could possibly be pregnant. I have been taking my birth control pills. I only skipped a few times, but I have been a little careless, having sex with Damien and not using a condom. I decided I needed to make an appointment with my doctor. I didn't want to alarm anyone, and I sure wasn't about to tell my mom. So I decided to go to the doctor by myself.

I sat there patiently waiting in the exam room for the doctor to read my results of the pregnancy test. In all actuality I hadn't even noticed I missed my period. Maybe I skipped more pills than I thought. I looked in my purse to see when did I take my last pill. As I searched through my purse I couldn't find the pills, and that's when I pulled out the refill prescription. How did I forget to get my pills refilled? What was I thinking I couldn't believe I let three weeks go by?

As the doctor walked in the room I froze. "Are you okay?" "Just a little nervous." "So why are

Once Damien put that promise ring on my finger, I felt like this was so real, I mean Damien had changed. He started to surprise me in ways I thought was never possible, and that night I was more open with him and we actually got high together. That night for once sex was so good, I don't know if it was because we didn't use a condom or the fact I was high. All I know was I would never forget this Valentines Day. This was truly a night to remember.

even have time for each other? What if they do me like I did them, and ignore our friendship or place it on hold. I needed to just quite tripping and worry about what's going on now.

I mean here I am finally having Damien being the romantic type, he cooked me a nice dinner, and even bought me six of the most beautiful roses, and now he is in the kitchen making me an ice cream sundae.

"Dang Damien, that looks good." "I knew you weren't fixing to pass this chocolate sundae up." "Do you think you have enough chocolate though?" "What it's only chocolate ice cream, chocolate chips, and chocolate syrup. Oh here's the spoon." As I reached to grab the spoon I noticed something around it. I glanced closely and saw that it was a ring.

"Before you get all crazy on me, it's just a promise ring." "Wow Damien I wasn't expecting this." "Meshay you know I love you, and when I'm ready to take that step I do want you to be the one I marry." "Damien we never even talked about it." "I didn't need to I know you the type of female that's wants marriage and a family."

to do a paper on teen suicide. I was starting to feel just why teens commit suicide. I needed to take a break, so I went to the restroom. I started to feel a little cramping. As I used the bathroom, I notice a slight bloody discharge on my panties. I was happy to know that my period had come down. I purchased a pad out the machine.

Finally a sign of relief, I no longer had to patiently wait for my results, and at this point I knew I probably wasn't pregnant. I still needed to hear from my doctor just to be sure. Once I did I couldn't wait to start my pills again; I may have to get the dosage increased. I really needed to be careful. I was lucky I could have been pregnant, and thank God I'm not; at least I hope not.

I'm Finished

This day has finally arrived, and I'm happy that I made it. Just dealing with my parents, the drama with Damien, and my pregnancy scare was more than enough to make me want to act a fool, but I dealt with it and now it seems I'm closing one chapter of my life and opening a new one. As I sat here at my graduation looking back at all I went through this past year, I was relieved that nothing came in between me finishing high school.

I felt things in my life were getting better, well not everything, of course, there was still the issue at hand as to if Damien had a baby, but the situation was working itself out and finally Tranay agreed to give him a blood test. I told Damien I would stick by him, although I really ain't trying to be a step mom to nobody at this point in my life, but I love Damien and I'm willing to do whatever it takes to keep our relationship strong. We overcame so much already. He even got a job coaching youth football.

I was looking forward to my new job and attending college in the fall. I thought I was going to have to wait until after graduation for my car, but my parents surprised me early. So now I have a brand new Honda Civic, a red one at that. Mechelle is even maturing only a little but it's a start she even got asked to her 8th grade ball. I actually volunteered to take her and pick her up.

I wanted it to be special, and for once I was showing my love for her, I drove Damien's car. Of course Mechelle was so excited. Who else was going to be pulling up in an old-school mustang, most of her friends were in limos but we still got a little hood in us, so of course I had to floss my sister around. I was excited that Damien even let me drive his car.

My parents gave me and my friends a big graduation party. It was more of a going away for Danielle; she decided to go out of state for college. I still promised to keep in touch and the first chance we got me and Shabria promised to fly out and see her. Shabria still was determined to leave home. Selena had broken up with Kevin and he moved out, but no sooner than he left she get another boyfriend, and Shabria swore this one was no different.

So from time to time, Shabria and Steven would stay at Shaun's place. Shabria said once she saved up enough money to move, she was out of there. She got a job at the Community Center. Shabria had more experience than me, she was into a lot of sports and her skills made her more qualified to work at the center. I was just happy we both made it, and both were fulfilling our dreams.

It goes to show you, no matter what your background is, where you came from, how you were raised, you can still achieve something out of life. If you put your mind to it and never give up, no matter how many obstacles are in your way. It also helps to have people stand by you. I had just that, my family and my friends, and I turned that around and used it to help my boyfriend see that despite his circumstances he could change, but only if he really wanted to.

For the most part things are good, they're not perfect, but at this moment I'm happy, I'm not stressed, angry, or even frustrated and tired, the way I was before. I'm learning to deal with them, I had no other choice because if things didn't get better, or I didn't learn how to handle them; I really would have Acted a Damn Fool.